My Bison

Princeton Architectural Press · New York

The first time I saw him, it was springtime.

I was walking in the tall grass.
My mother picked me up so that I could see him.
"Look!" she said. "He's back!"

Every day I returned to
the same place.

Every day, I got closer, and he let me.
Once I thought I heard him murmur, "Come near."

I was no longer just any human to him.
I brought him things to eat. "I made it myself!"
He didn't always like my food, but he always tasted it,
which made me happy.

My bison left one morning.
I wished he could have stayed,
but he had to join up with
the other bison.
I walked with him until it was
time to say goodbye.
He looked at me for a long
while, and then he was gone.
But I knew he'd be back
when snow covered the
ground again.

How lonely it was without him.

But before long, it was winter again.

I knew the moment he returned. I could feel it.

The earth trembled.

My friend was back!

We settled down by the fire.
My bison listened with tenderness as
I told him stories.

I told him stories about the forest I loved,
and all the things I'd done while he was gone.

Sometimes he wouldn't say anything.

I loved his silence.

I loved his frozen nose.

I loved his breath.

Being with my bison kept me warm.

I loved him completely.

Year after year, my bison returned.

He never noticed I was getting older. He was too.

We were never cold in the snow.

Once, we talked all night,
and I remembered how my mother,
so long ago, had held me up
to see him for the first time.

I told him about how she used to make me
hot chocolate when I couldn't sleep.
She taught me the songs of birds and how
to find my way with the stars.

I missed her so much.

"And you, my bison, do you remember your mother,
her sweet smell, and snuggling in her soft, warm fur?
I bet you miss her so much."

And then one winter, my bison didn't come.

I looked for him for a long time.

In the forest, I felt like a little girl again.

But I didn't find him.

That night, I came home with a heavy heart.
The sky was bright with stars, more than I had ever seen
before. I cried. I missed my bison so much.

And then I felt him by my side.

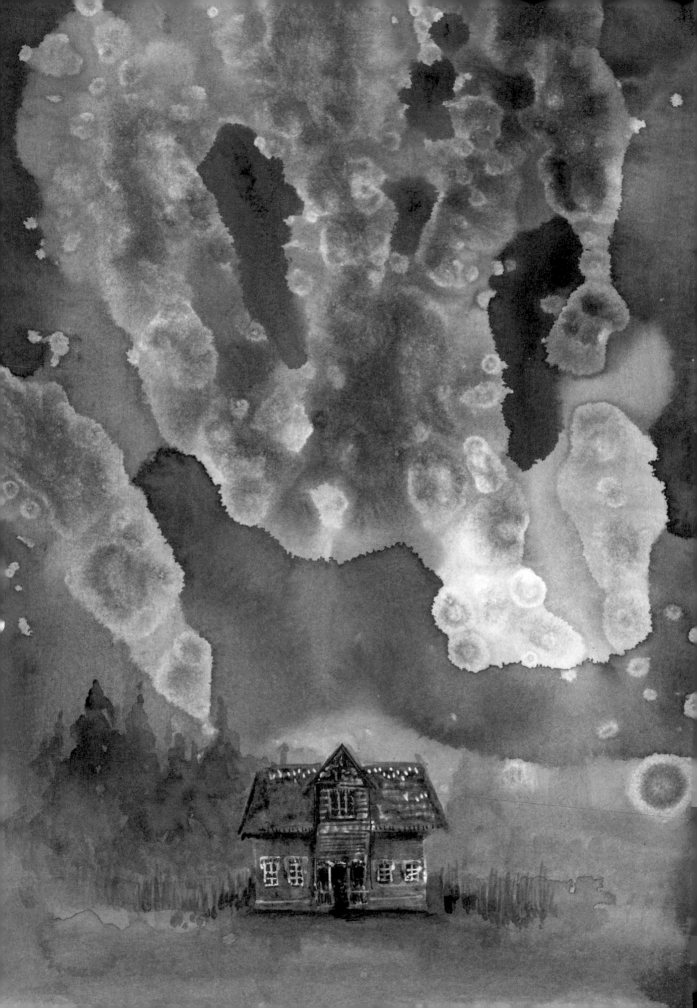

And in my heart I heard him say,
"I am in every spring flower, every sound in the forest,
and every snowflake."

He was always with me.
He had never left.